GW01144884

Holly the Elf
A Christmas Tale

Written by

J.T. Grainger

Illustrated by

Omnia Tulba

Cali-FLY Books
Indianapolis

Holly the Elf: A Christmas Tale

Written by J.T. Grainger
Illustrated by Omnia Tulba
Edited by Helen Million & Melissa Tuck

Copyright © 2021 by J.T. Grainger

All rights reserved. No part of this book may be reproduced or transmitted in any form or by any means without written permission of the author.

Published by Cali-FLY Books, P.O. Box 421063, Indianapolis, IN 46242 USA

ISBN: E-Book: 978-1-956993-02-8
ISBN: Softcover: 978-1-956993-01-1
ISBN: Hardcover: 978-1-956993-00-4

Printed in the United States of America

First printing, November 2021

There are a lot of stories about the North Pole. Many of them have to do with Santa Claus and a sleigh full of wondrous toys. Some of them mention his wife, Mrs. Claus. Some of them talk about his flying reindeer — one of which has a glowing red nose. But, until now, no one outside of the North Pole has ever heard the tale of Holly the Elf.

For the 364 days prior to Christmas, Santa's workshop is always filled with jolly little elves preparing for Christmas Eve.

In the past, the larger elves would carry wood and all sorts of other materials and the smaller elves would help carve or mold these materials to make special toys for good little girls and boys. Together, these elves were known as "Builders" and they were responsible for creating each and every toy at Santa's shop.

Once the Builders were finished making the toys, they were placed on a long cart and taken to another group of eager elves.

These elves were called "Inspectors". It was their job to test each one and make sure they were safe for children around the world. Batons were twirled, balls were bounced and dolls were cuddled. Needless to say, it could be very tiring work, but the merry little elves were always up to the task.

After each toy had passed inspection, they were collected once more and taken to yet another area of the workshop. This area was known as the "Gift Wrapping Department". It was there that every single present was carefully wrapped with bright bows, colorful paper and a special name tag for each and every child on Santa's list. Then, they were placed inside Santa's bag to be delivered on Christmas Eve by the jolly man himself.

You see, this was always how Santa's workshop had functioned. Every single elf had been given a specific job to do and no elf was ever asked, or expected, to do anything different. For years and years, this arrangement had worked. Yet, little did these elves know, things at the North Pole were about to change.

It all started December 23 — the day before Christmas Eve. The workshop was running like clockwork. Builders were building toys, Inspectors were inspecting toys and the Gift Wrapping Department was making each toy special with final, thoughtful touches.

Holly the Elf was busy wrapping a toy car, when suddenly, she heard a loud —

KAAAAAAAAA-POP!

Then, a thin cloud of grey smoke began to rise into the air from the partially wrapped gift.

"Oh, no!" Holly exclaimed as she put the car down and fanned the toy with her hand. "It must be broken. But, how could that be?"

It didn't make sense. Holly had never seen a toy do that before.

"Could it be the batteries?" she thought, grabbing a new pair. "Maybe they just need to be changed?"

It was worth a shot. However, putting new batteries in the car didn't seem to help because the stubborn toy refused to turn on or make another sound.

"Oh, what's wrong with you, you silly car?!" Holly sighed in frustration.

She was about to give up and toss the toy aside, but then, she decided to go and speak with the Builder elves to see if they could repair it.

"Yes," she said to herself on the way over to talk to them. "I'm sure they'll know just how to fix it."

It was a good idea, but when Holly tried to show the Builder elves the toy car, they refused to help.

"It's not our job to inspect toys," one said.

"We don't do that sort of thing here," said a second.

"We can only build you a new one," said a third.

"No, we can't," said a fourth elf. "We don't have time for that. It's almost Christmas Eve and there are still many other toys left to be finished."

Holly was disheartened by this news. To her, it seemed like there was something very special about the tiny toy car, but no matter what she said, the Builder elves wouldn't listen.

With her head hung low, Holly thanked the busy elves and started back to her gift wrapping area. Then, all of a sudden, an idea occurred to her.

"Perhaps I should show it to the Inspectors?" Holly thought as she stood there scratching her head. "After all, it is their job to test each toy before it reaches the Gift Wrapping Department. Somehow, this toy was missed. Maybe if I show it to the Inspectors, they'll want to do something about it!"

However, just like the Builders, the Inspector elves refused to help.

"It's not possible," said one.

"There's barely any time left to repair it," said a second.

"You'd be better off with a new car," said a third. "And, we don't do that sort of thing here."

"Perhaps you should try the Builders?" suggested a fourth elf.

Once more, Holly was filled with sadness. It really seemed like there was something very special about the tiny toy car, but no matter what she said, the Inspector elves wouldn't listen.

In defeat, Holly thanked the group of elves and started off again to her gift wrapping area.

Then, a third idea sprang to mind.

"Maybe I could fix it myself?" she thought. "If I work all night, it might be done by Christmas Eve."

But unfortunately, Holly had only worked in the Gift Wrapping Department. And so, she had no idea how to repair one.

"No, that won't work," she told herself. "You don't know the first thing about fixing toy cars or even where to start. Besides, even if you try, there's probably no way you'll ever finish in time."

Right then, Holly felt yet another wave of despair. To the poor elf, everything seemed hopeless. But, just as she was about to give up, she had another thought.

"Santa's library!" she remembered suddenly. "There are lots of wonderful books in there. Maybe one of them can tell me how to fix the toy car!"

In Santa's library, Holly found dozens of books on toy-making. There were ones about sculpting wooden figurines, building dollhouses, constructing model train sets and even one about creating and repairing battery-powered toy cars.

Hastily, Holly read the book from cover to cover then went back to her area in the Gift Wrapping Department.

With renewed confidence, she set to work on the broken toy car using the tools she had on hand.

Holly didn't eat. She didn't sleep. She just kept working and working on the toy car. By the time she looked up at the clock on her wall, it was already morning. Time felt like it had gone by in the blink of an eye.

"Goodness!" she exclaimed in astonishment. "Why, it's Christmas Eve! I'll never be able to finish repairs in time!"

Holly was filled with hopelessness. To the small elf, there didn't seem to be anything else she could do to fix the car before Santa's big flight. Then suddenly, an idea dawned on her.

"Santa!" she thought with delight. "I must go and see Santa! He knows all about toys. Surely he will help me fix this in time!"

So, grabbing the toy car, Holly made her way over to see Santa.

The sun was barely up as Holly trudged along the path leading to Santa's house. All around her, everything was covered in brilliant, powdery white snow. And faintly, in the distance, she could still hear the sound of hundreds and hundreds of elves at work.

"Welcome, Holly!" Santa said, greeting her with a big, warm smile. "Merry Christmas, my dear!"

"Merry Christmas, Santa," Holly replied as she held up the toy car for him to inspect. "I was hoping you could take a look at this? I came across it yesterday while I was wrapping presents. For some reason, it doesn't work. I showed it to the other elves, but no one could help me fix it. Is there anything you can do?"

"Hmm…" Santa said, eyeing the toy curiously. "You say it doesn't work?"

"Yes," Holly replied sadly. "It won't light up or make any sound. I've tried everything I could think of to fix it. First, I gave it new batteries. Then, I read a book about toy-making from your library and spent all night trying to repair it myself, but nothing has worked."

Carefully, she placed the tiny toy in Santa's giant hands and watched eagerly as he studied it.

At first, the wise and jolly old man did not say a word. He merely turned the toy over and flipped its power button on. Instantly, the toy car revved to life. Its miniature headlights glowed, its wheels began to turn and its small motor made a loud humming noise.

"Hmm," he said, starting to chuckle. "It seems to work just fine now. Why, I'd say, it is as good as new, my dear. Well done!"

Holly didn't know what to make of it. Had she been so tired from working all night that she had forgotten to switch the car on that morning? Yes, apparently so.

At that moment, she couldn't help but feel a little foolish. After all, it was the day before Christmas. Santa had a very important job to do that night and the last thing Holly wanted to do was bother him or cause delay from his last minute Christmas Eve duties.

"I am so sorry, Santa," Holly said with remorse. "I should have rechecked the toy before coming here. I had no idea it was working now. I know you're extremely busy and I didn't mean to waste your time."

"Waste my time?" Santa repeated, before letting out a deep and joyous laugh. "Why, my dear child, you could never waste my time! I am so glad you came to visit, Holly. You see, before you arrived, I had been going over my list to make sure that each and every present would be ready by tonight. I even looked it over a second time. But, for some strange reason, there was one toy missing — this toy car. I feared that a deserving child would not get a gift from me this year."

"Oh, no!" Holly exclaimed in astonishment.

"Yes," Santa agreed. "Thanks to you, my dear, it looks like now — no child on my list will be missed! You know, perhaps it is time you do more than wrap presents at the workshop? It's no secret that the Builder elves and the Inspector elves have certainly felt a little overwhelmed lately. Do you think you could give them a hand?"

"Oh yes, Santa," Holly replied with a bright, rosy grin. "Nothing would please me more. Though, I don't see why I can't help both the Inspectors AND the Builders? After all, I do believe each job is equally important."

Santa seemed to think long and hard about Holly's answer. He had to admit she had a very good point. Why was each job at the workshop separate from the other?

"You're right," he finally said. "ALL jobs are equally important. Therefore, neither you nor any of the other elves shall ever have to choose between them. For, let it be known, that beginning Christmas Day, any elf who desires to do more than one job at the workshop is perfectly welcome to do so."

"They are?!" Holly proclaimed in astonishment.

"Yes, my dear, they are," Santa answered warmly. "However, there is just one more thing, Holly. After I make my deliveries tonight, I would like you to come and help me run things around the workshop for a while."

"Me, Santa?" Holly asked in bewilderment. "But, why me?"

"Well..." Santa revealed. "I suspect it's going to take a very special elf to manage these changes in the workshop and make sure that what —almost— happened this Christmas... never happens again. I also have reason to believe that this special elf is you, Holly. So, what do you say, my dear? Will you help me?"

"Why, yes, of course, Santa!" Holly replied. "It would be an absolute honor to help in any way that I can."

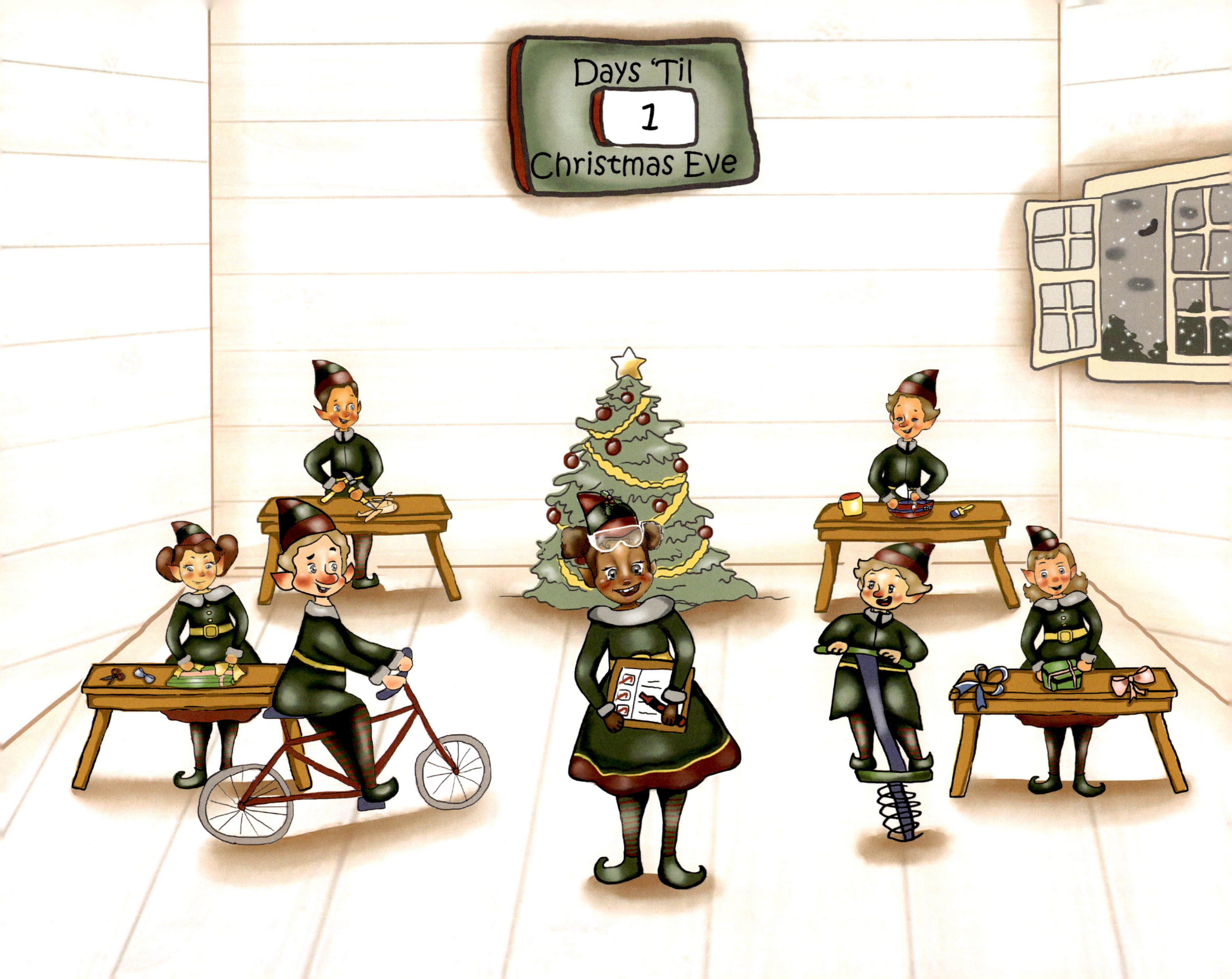
Days 'Til
1
Christmas Eve

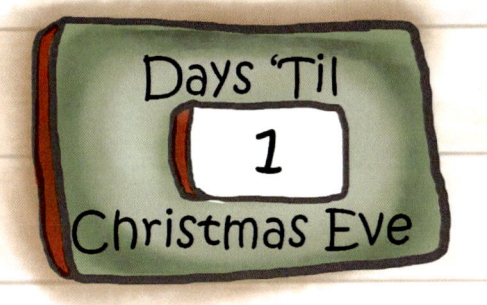

And so, from that day forward, Holly became the most trusted elf in Santa's workshop. Under her skillful leadership, each gift was made with precision and care and no toy was ever discarded or abandoned.

Every year, each elf who works at Santa's shop builds, inspects and wraps each present.

And, every year, Santa recounts the tale of Holly the Elf. The spirited elf— whose determination and joy— ensured that there was something special for every little good girl and boy.

THE END

Holly the Elf

Piano Ver.

J.T. Grainger

Lento

There are so many stories— A— bout the North Pole. But, there's one more Christmas tale, that you

♩ = 176
Swing

oughta know— Holly worked at San—ta's Shop, wrap—ping Christmas

pre — sents. Then one day, she heard a noise that didn't sou—nd too plea—sant.

Smoke was pourin' out of a toy, just like a corn cob pipe. So, she spoke to the

other elves— To see if they could make it right. Oh, poor Holly the Elf— Just a

Lightning Source UK Ltd.
Milton Keynes UK
UKRC051126301121
394856UK00001B/5